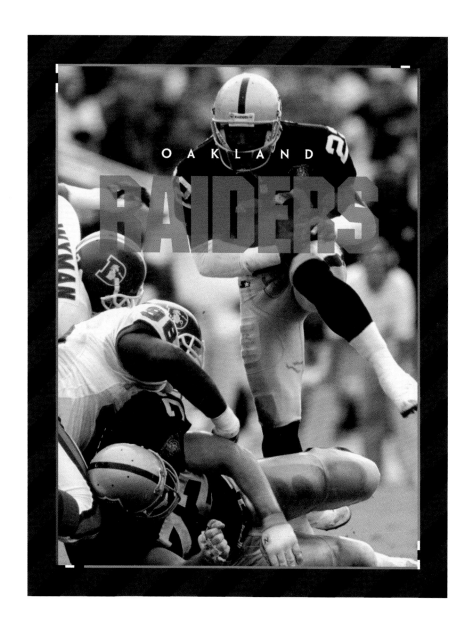

OAKLAND RAIDERS

STEVE POTTS

CREATIVE 🍎 EDUCATION

Published by Creative Education
123 South Broad Street, Mankato, Minnesota 56001
Creative Education is an imprint of The Creative Company

Designed by Rita Marshall
Cover illustration by Rob Day

Photos by: Allsport Photography, Associated Press, Bettmann Archive,
Duomo, Fotosport, FPG International, and SportsChrome.

Library of Congress Cataloging-in-Publication Data

Potts, Steve, 1956-
Oakland Raiders / by Steve Potts.
p. cm. — (NFL Today)
Summary: Traces the history of the team from its beginnings through 1996.
ISBN 0-88682-800-7

1. Oakland Raiders (Football team)—History—Juvenile literature.
[1. Oakland Raiders (Football team) 2. Football—History.]
I. Title. II. Series.

GV956.O24P68   1996   96-15245
796.332'64'0979466—dc20

123456

In sports equipment stores throughout America, some of the most popular t-shirts, hats and jerseys are silver and black—colors worn by the Oakland Raiders. From California to New York, from Florida to Oregon, fans support the Raiders because they are winners.

The Raiders have been an important part of pro football since the 1960s. Entering their 25th year in 1995, they topped all National Football League franchises with a .657 winning percentage. They are also the only team to play in Super Bowls in the 1960s, 1970s and 1980s. The first time they made the playoffs, in 1967, the Raiders also went to the Super Bowl. Theirs is a championship tradition.

Gus Otto (#34) and Dave Grayson helped make the Raiders great.

1 9 6 1

Center Jim Otto was selected to the AFL's All-League team for the second straight year.

Al Davis is the man behind the Raiders organization. Since he took over the losing team in 1963, his hard work, spirit and energy have taken Oakland to the top.

Davis began his pro football career as an assistant coach with the San Diego Chargers. While at San Diego, he helped make the Chargers into one of the most feared passing teams in football.

A challenge waited for Al Davis in Oakland, and the young coach moved there in 1963 to take over the floundering Oakland Raiders. Oakland, the last club to get an AFL franchise, was starving for good players and good leadership. People said the Raiders had three teams: one going, one coming and one already there. Players joined the Raiders on Monday and would be gone by Saturday. One player who was a steady presence went on to become a legend: Jim Otto. Many Raiders fans remember his name, but they also remember him by his number "00."

One of the original players in the Raiders' first training camp, Otto immediately became a team leader. The 6-foot-2, 255-pound center played college ball for the University of Miami. Some veteran NFL players couldn't believe that such a talented player would sign with an AFL team. "I could make some NFL clubs I know," said Otto, "but it's more of an honor and distinction to be an original member of a brand new league. That's why I chose to play with the Oakland Raiders." There wasn't much honor or success for Otto during the team's first three seasons. The Raiders won only nine of their 33 games in 1960, 1961 and 1962. Players and fans alike searched for answers to their team's poor showing.

Running back Harvey Williams sparked the offense in the 1990s (page 7).

The Raiders needed some inspiration, and it came with 34-year-old Al Davis. Davis came to Oakland filled with energy and new ideas. "Poise is the secret," Davis told his team. "No matter what the scoreboard says, keep your poise." In 1963, his first season, the Raiders rocketed to a 10-4 record, narrowly missing the AFL playoffs.

Other team owners in the AFL noticed Davis's winning attitude. The new league, created in 1960, was battling the NFL for fan loyalty throughout the country. To give the AFL the edge in this battle, the team owners made Davis the commissioner of the American Football League in April 1966.

Davis resigned from his job eight weeks later, after putting an end to the six-year struggle between the AFL and NFL. The two leagues became one expanded league. Davis was considered the man behind the settlement. The merger completed, Davis returned to the Raiders as general manager. Although his coaching career was over, he had another goal in mind: making the Raiders into world champions.

1 9 6 8

Coach Al Davis led the Raiders to more wins than in the previous two years combined.

A COMMITMENT TO EXCELLENCE

With the two leagues united, a true world champion could now be crowned, and the Raiders wanted that crown. On January 14, 1968, in the second NFL-AFL Super Bowl, the Raiders met the mighty Green Bay Packers, coached by legendary Vince Lombardi.

"Seven years ago I thought this day would never come," Jim Otto said proudly. "We are in the Super Bowl." Other much older teams had never made it this far. The Raiders had achieved so much in only seven years—from playing games on a high school field during their opening season all the way to the world championship showdown.

In the Super Bowl, Raiders coach John Rauch tried several strategies, but his young team was no match for Lombardi's veterans. The game ended with a 33-14 Green Bay win.

Three years after their first Super Bowl appearance, the decade ended with the Raiders established as one of pro football's best teams. Many players, including Bill Miller, George Blanda, Fred Biletnikoff, Willie Brown and Daryle Lamonica, made Oakland a strong contender. While the decade began with a losing record, it ended in 1969 with a startling 12-1-1 season for Oakland.

Fiery head coach John Madden led the Raiders to a 10-3-1 record and the play-offs.

The Raiders continued to dominate during their second decade. A burly new coach brought a new era to Raiders football in the 1970s. That new coach, John Madden, rewrote the book on effective coaching style in the NFL.

Most coaches were strong disciplinarians who treated players like animals. Madden used an emotional approach. "I had a philosophy," Madden explained. "I really liked my players. I liked them as people. I made a point to talk to each player personally every day." Madden brought fun to the game.

"I think some coaches get hung up on power," Madden reflected. "They forget that football is still a game of people and it's supposed to be fun. You can be intense and competitive and all that, but try to remember to laugh and have fun. It's just a football game."

Madden instilled this philosophy in his team. Not only did they have fun, they also won. Madden's team became famous for snatching victories in unusual ways with remarkable players. One of these magicians was Ken "the Snake" Stabler, Oakland's powerful left-handed quarterback.

Defensive end Howie Long was an All-Pro in the 1980s (pages 10-11).

Stabler won his nickname in high school after zigzagging across the football field like a snake as he returned a punt for a touchdown. Stabler grew up in football country—Foley, Alabama—and quarterbacked Bear Bryant's University of Alabama team.

As the Raiders quarterback, Stabler's greatest asset was his quick release. In 1972, he led the league in passing and Oakland remained the team to beat. Their 10-3-1 record that season landed them in the playoffs. They were seconds away from beating Pittsburgh when Franco Harris pulled off his famous "Immaculate Reception" play to seal a 13-7 Pittsburgh win in the first round.

In 1973, the Raiders were back. Stabler and a powerful Oakland defense led the team to a 9-4-1 record. This time, the Raiders got revenge against Pittsburgh when they thrashed the Steelers 33-14 in the playoffs. But Don Shula's Miami Dolphins came

between the Raiders and the Super Bowl. Miami beat the Raiders in the AFC championship game 27-10.

Madden and his Raiders just couldn't get over that last winning hurdle. For three years (1973-1975) they ended up in the playoffs but failed to take the championship. As the 1976 season began, fans wondered whether the Raiders would ever make a breakthrough. Al Davis gave Madden his vote of confidence and Madden placed his future in Ken Stabler's hands. When reporters asked Stabler about the Raiders' past failures, Stabler answered, "Last year don't mean beans to me. It's this year that counts." With help from receivers like Dave Casper, Cliff Branch and Fred Biletnikoff, Stabler was ready for the season.

The Raiders pledged a total organizational effort to get the team into the Super Bowl. Everyone in Oakland, fans included, seemed determined to make 1976 the Raiders' season. In one game after another, nothing seemed to be able to stop the Raiders. Effortlessly, it seemed, Oakland pressed its way through the regular season and their first playoff game. Their incredible dedication had thus far paid off.

As the AFC championship game approached, though, it looked as if history might repeat itself. Oakland faced the Pittsburgh Steelers, the team that three times had ended the Raiders' march toward the Super Bowl. In 1976, however, Oakland crushed the overmatched Steelers 27-7. Wild Oakland fans realized that only one more team, the Minnesota Vikings, stood in the way of Oakland's championship dreams.

Minnesota, featuring the renowned "Purple People Eaters" defensive front row, were indeed a team to be feared as the Super Bowl began. But Oakland had a secret weapon: Fred Biletnikoff. This outstanding receiver snatched three key long passes to set up three Oakland touchdowns. Biletnikoff was

Veteran wide receiver Fred Biletnikoff caught 43 passes for 551 yards and seven touchdowns.

13

Jim Plunkett won the starting quarterback position and threw 18 touchdown passes.

named the Super Bowl Most Valuable Player for his heroics. And the Raiders walked off the field with their first Super Bowl victory, a 34-14 drubbing of the Vikings. At last John Madden, the coach whom George Blanda had called "the kindest and most thoughtful coach I ever had," got the Super Bowl ring he had long strived for.

Madden and his recharged Raiders failed in their attempt to win back to back Super Bowls, their hopes frustrated in 1978 by the Denver Broncos. As many of his fellow coaches had discovered, Madden found that the high level of quality amongst conference competitions made it difficult to retain the AFC championship year after year.

THE TRADITION CONTINUES

John Madden decided in 1978 that he wanted to make a move into sports broadcasting and left the Raiders with a career 103-32-7 record, including seven division titles and a Super Bowl victory. Madden and Al Davis ensured that the transition to a new coach would move ahead quickly. When Tom Flores was chosen as Oakland's new skipper, he found a team eager to climb the heights again to victory.

Like many other students of the game, Flores knew about Oakland's reputation as a place where the game's outcasts, troublemakers and aged veterans ended their careers. When he came in as coach he found Jim Plunkett, one such former star, sitting on the bench.

Plunkett was one of those promising college players who turned pro and never lived up to that promise. Plunkett played well for New England, but then spent several years trailing from one team to another. Flores thought he detected a spark of the

Rookie Marcus Allen became a star touchdown runner in the 1980s.   15

ambition and talent that once drove Plunkett, so he put his faith in the veteran quarterback. What followed was simply one of the most amazing personal comebacks in football history.

After the Raiders lost three of their first five games in 1980, Flores figured he had little to lose. He sent Plunkett in. His faith wasn't misplaced. Plunkett quarterbacked his team to nine wins in their next 11 games. By season's end, the Raiders made the playoffs as a Wild Card team.

Reaching the Super Bowl is no easy walk for any team, but the Wild Card team has another obstacle in their path: they have to play on the road and they have to play one game more than anyone else. At the end of a tough regular season, this combination can hurt the best of teams. The Raiders rose to the opportunity and made themselves the first Wild Card team to make it to the Super Bowl.

A popular target of Jim Plunkett's, running back Frank Hawkins.

Tight end Todd Christensen caught 42 passes.

Many sports commentators didn't give Oakland much of a chance of winning, but Plunkett and the Raiders defense, led by cornerback Lester Hayes, went into Super Bowl XV determined to win. Plunkett completed 13 of 21 passes, including three touchdown passes, in Oakland's 27-10 win over the Philadelphia Eagles. One of Plunkett's touchdown passes was the incredible 80-yard bullet to Kenny King that set a Super Bowl record. When the Raiders left the field in New Orleans that day, no one doubted that they deserved the Super Bowl championship.

The 1982 draft brought Heisman Trophy winner Marcus Allen, a running back from USC, to Oakland. Allen, who would go on to set team records for rushing and total touchdowns, seemed just the offensive weapon Plunkett needed to balance the passing attack. It appeared that the Raiders had produced a com-

bination that would lead them to further championship glory in the 1980s.

1 9 8 3

Rookie defensive end Greg Townsend went on to become an All-Pro in the late 1980s.

THE RAIDERS HEAD SOUTH

There was another major change in 1982. The Raiders decided to leave their home in Oakland to move south to Los Angeles. The Raiders loved Oakland, but their stadium only sat 50,000 fans. Davis believed that his team could draw at least 90,000 fans per game in Los Angeles, and profits won out over loyalty to Oakland fans. After bringing a court case against the NFL because they were trying to block his move, Davis took his team south for the 1982 season.

Once the Raiders were situated in their new home, they kicked off the 1982 season with three straight wins. The team found that Marcus Allen, who had played college football just down the road while at USC, was an attraction who drew fans to the new team in town. Allen rushed for 697 yards in his rookie year, averaging 5.7 yards per carry and tallying 14 touchdowns. It was no surprise to Raiders fans that Allen was named Rookie of the Year.

Marcus Allen disappointed some fans in 1983, though he still led the team in rushing. Even if Allen's critics thought he was having an off-year, no one could say the same about his team. Led by a brilliant offensive line, the Raiders carried a 12-4 record into the post-season, which they rode all the way to the Super Bowl. In that ultimate championship spotlight, Allen turned in a performance that devastated both the opposing Washington Redskins and his hometown critics. When the Raiders had faced Washington earlier in the year, they had lost to the Redskins

Defensive end Howie Long played with great intensity.

in a closely-fought 37-35 struggle. This time, however, the Raiders offense was ready for the supposedly powerful Redskins, while the Raiders defense limited the Redskins to only one touchdown and one field goal enroute to one of the most lopsided victories in Super Bowl history. When the buzzer signaled the game's end, the Raiders exulted over their 38-9 victory. Marcus Allen had pummeled the Washington defense, carrying the ball 20 times for a record 191 yards. In the third quarter he turned in two touchdown runs, one of them a 74-yard jaunt that made the Super Bowl recordbook. Raiders right guard Mickey Marvin remembered seeing Allen rush by him on his famous run. "I was picking myself up off the ground," Marvin said, "then I looked around and a rocket went through!" The rocket, of course, was the speedy Allen rushing toward the Washington goal line. Allen commented after the game that "this has to be the greatest feeling of my life. I've been to the Rose Bowl. I've won the Heisman Trophy. But nothing is sweeter than this."

Art Shell replaced Mike Shanahan as head coach in mid-season—and posted a 7-5 record.

THE RAIDERS' PRIDE AND POWER

Greatness arrives only so often. But with the Raiders, it had come to seem like an everyday occurrence. So when things went wrong, everybody was surprised. Such a surprise came in 1988, after the Raiders had missed the playoffs for two consecutive years.

After coach Tom Flores retired, Al Davis brought in Denver Broncos assistant Mike Shanahan to direct the ship. But Shanahan lasted only four games. The fact that Shanahan was new to the ways of the Raiders franchise was part of the problem.

Raiders seemed to understand Raiders. "Once a Raider, always," said former defensive end Otis Sistrunk. "We are close.

Left to right: Lionel Washington, Marcus Allen, Willie Gault, Bo Jackson.

Whenever I meet a Raider today, I don't just say hello and give a handshake. I hug and kiss him."

In an attempt to recapture this feeling, Davis chose offensive line coach Art Shell to replace Shanahan as head coach. Shell, named to the Hall of Fame in 1989, had Raiders blood running through his veins. He coached the team until 1994. Many Raiders fans think Shell was the best offensive tackle to ever play the game. He went to the Pro Bowl eight times, a Raiders record, and played in 207 league games, an impressive total over fifteen seasons. One of the most respected men in football, Shell's players knew that they could trust him.

Speedy and powerful, Bo Jackson ran the ball for 5.6 yards per carry.

A winning NFL coach, however, needs more than just respect. He needs talented, disciplined and hardworking players. One man on Shell's roster epitomized those characteristics more than any other player: Bo Jackson.

Vincent Edward Jackson was born in Bessemer, Alabama. Wild as a youngster, he was the eighth of ten children. His brothers and sisters described him as being wild as a "boarhog." His nickname "Bo" came from boarhog's abbreviated version, "bo 'hog."

Everyone knew Bo was a great talent. He won the Heisman Trophy in 1985 as a running back for Auburn. The Tampa Bay Buccaneers made him their number one pick in the NFL Draft in 1985. Instead of joining the Buccaneers, however, Jackson chose a second option—signing a pro baseball contract with the Kansas City Royals. Two years later, Al Davis chose Jackson as a seventh round draft choice. He was the 183rd player taken. Many sports observers thought Davis had made a bad choice. No one, they thought, could play two professional sports in the same season.

Howie Long specialized in sacking the opposing quarterback (pages 26-27).

The sports world was anxious to see if Bo would measure up. Could he survive his rigorous schedule as a baseball player and come back to win at football? Critics didn't have to wait long to find out that Bo could play, and play well. In a Monday night game against Seattle, with all of America watching, Bo ran for an astonishing 221 yards, including a breathtaking 90-yard run. For his many accomplishments, Bo was named Rookie of the Year by *Football Digest*. By the time he left the Raiders—due to injuries—in 1990, Bo had compiled an impressive record. And due to his numerous television commercial appearances, the expression "Bo knows" was one of America's most famous phrases.

1 9 9 1

Raiders quarterback Jeff Hostetler provides veteran leadership for youthful Raiders offense.

THE RAIDERS IN THE 1990s

During Art Shell's five-year coaching stint, the Raiders made the playoffs in 1990, 1991 and again in 1993. Then, in 1994, the Raiders came closer to a Super Bowl berth, beating Denver 42-24 to win the AFC Wild Card game. But the Raiders saw their hopes of a return visit to the Super Bowl disappear when they journeyed to Buffalo. The Bills, playing on the coldest day in their history, pulled off a 29-23 victory over the Raiders. Raiders players had a hard time adjusting from southern California's warm weather to Buffalo's frigid winter. Few of them looked at the weather with the same sense of humor that Buffalo defensive end Bruce Smith had: "It's mind over matter. If you don't mind, it doesn't matter." Unfortunately for the Raiders, it did matter.

The Raiders took a significant step in their franchise history when they decided, in 1995, to return to their home turf of Oakland after a 13-year absence. That same year they hired

Guard Steve Winsniewski was a perennial All-Pro in the 1990s.

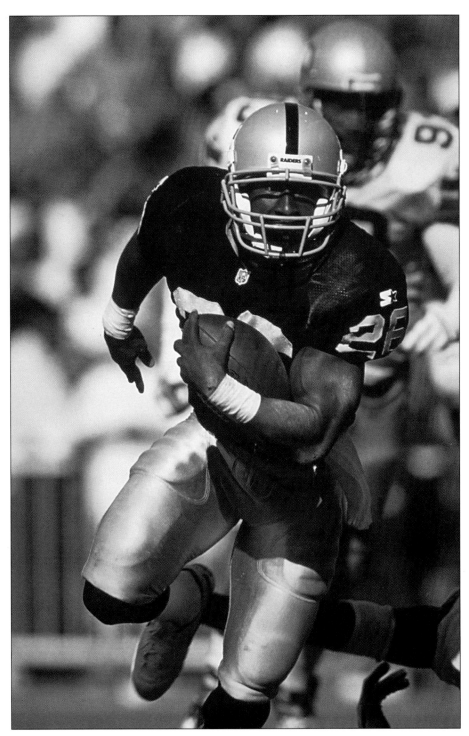

Rookie running back Napoleon Kaufman showed promise in 1995.

Cornerback Terry McDaniel intercepted seven passes in 1994.

Defensive tackle Russell Maryland is a fearsome presence when rushing opposing quarterbacks.

Mike White, a Raiders assistant coach, to act as the team's helmsman. With many years of college and professional experience, White seemed an excellent choice to return the new Oakland Raiders to football predominance.

The Raiders finished the 1995 season with an 8-8 record, a respectable showing in a tough division. Their final season game, a frustrating 31-28 loss to Denver, was the sixth loss in a row for first-year coach White. Oakland fans, though, were just glad to have their beloved Raiders back home. The Raiders and their fans hope to see Oakland's team again become the AFC's football powerhouse.